Brick by Brick

Seasons

Sandy Creek
NEW YORK

Spring

Rain cloud

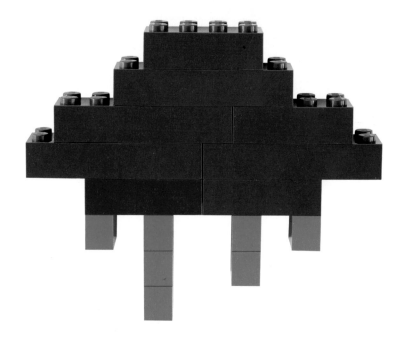

7 x 4 x 4 x

Sun and cloud

Frog

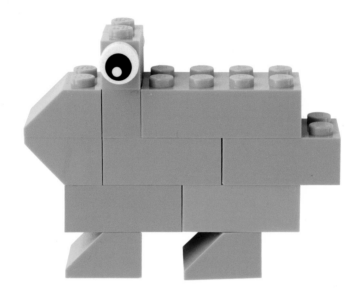

3 x 🔲 1 x 🔲 2 x ⚫ 2 x 🔲

4 x 🔲 1 x 🔲 1 x 🔲

Bird's nest

1x

2x   3x   3x   2x

Green leaf

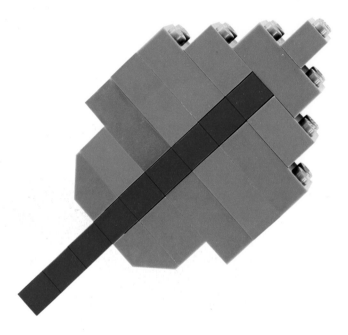

9 x  1 x

2 x 4 x 7 x

Spring blossoms

1x 🟡 4x ⬜

6x ⬜ 9x 🟫 4x 🟫

Flower

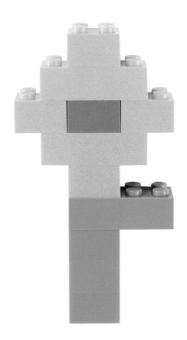

4 x 3 x

2 x 1 x 1 x

Rabbit

2 x 🧱 7 x 🧱 1 x 🧱 2 x 🧱

2 x 🧱 2 x 🧱 2 x ◉ 2 x 🧱

Chick

3 x ⬜ 1 x ⬜ 2 x ⬜

2 x ⬤ 2 x ⬜ 3 x ⬜ 2 x ⬜

2 x ⬜ 2 x ⬜ 1 x ⬜

Lamb

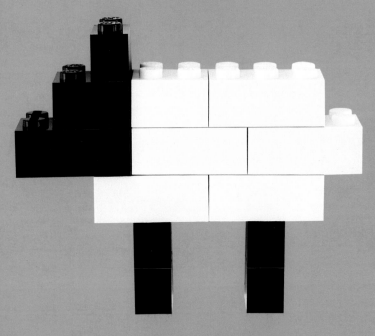

5 x 🧱 1 x 🧱

1 x 🧱 5 x 🧱 1 x 🧱

Summer

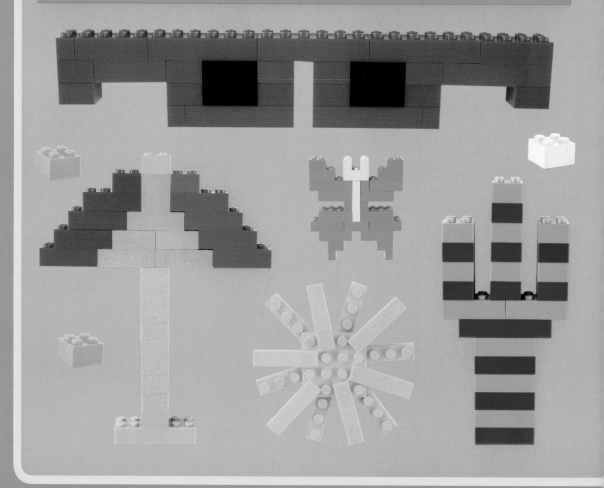

Sun

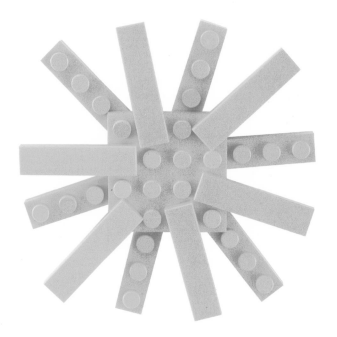

6 x ━━━ **6 x** ▭▭ **1 x** ▦

Popsicle

2 x 1 x 1 x 5 x

1 x 8 x 1 x 8 x

Beach umbrella

2 x 🟨 4 x 🟥 3 x 🟨 2 x 🟨

4 x 🟦 1 x ⬜ 10 x ⬜ 2 x 🟨 1 x 🟥

Sandcastle

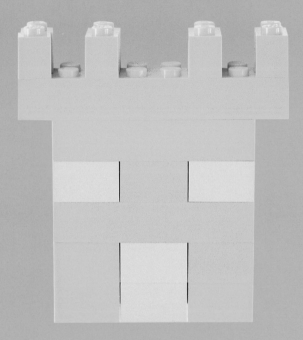

5 x 4 x 2 x

1 x 4 x

Butterfly

1 x   6 x

6 x   10 x   3 x   4 x

Green tree

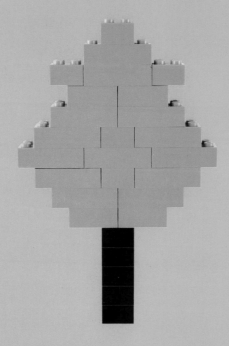

5 x 🟩 13 x 🟩 4 x 🟩 5 x ⬛

Cactus

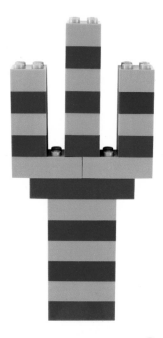

1 x

7 x   7 x   5 x   3 x

Corn on the cob

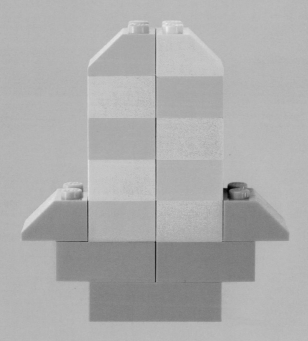

2 x 🟦 2 x 🟦 4 x 🟦

4 x 🟦 1 x 🟦 1 x 🟦 1 x 🟦

Sunglasses

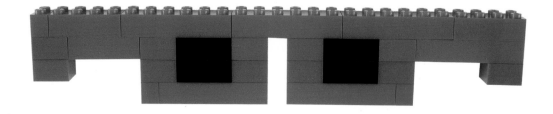

4 x 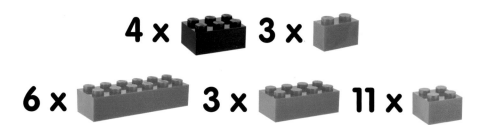 3 x

6 x 3 x 11 x

Lighthouse

8 x  2 x 6 x

2 x 1 x 1 x 2 x

2 x 2 x 3 x

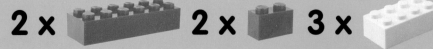

Rosebud

Cherries

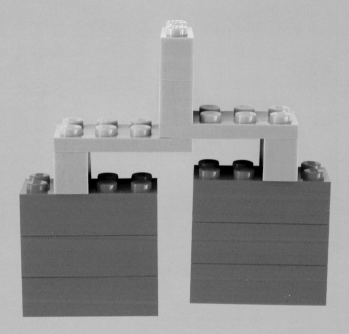

6 x   4 x   2 x

Fall

Rain boot

1x 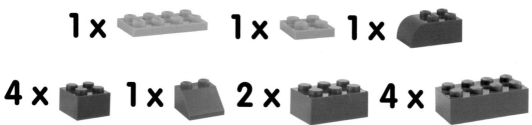 1x 1x

4x 1x 2x 4x

Raindrop

5 x 3 x 1 x

2 x 1 x

Jack o' lantern

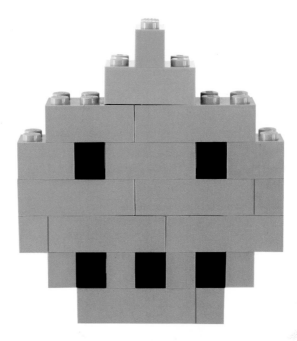

7 x   5 x   6 x   2 x

1 x   1 x   2 x

Falling leaves

9 x  4 x 11 x

Umbrella

1x  7x  1x

3x  3x  4x

Fall leaf

9 x  1 x 1 x 1 x

5 x 5 x 1 x 3 x

Acorn

1 x 🔲 2 x 🔲 3 x 🔲

2 x 🔲 2 x 🔲 2 x 🔲

Squirrel

1x ⬛ 2x ⬛ 1x ⬛

2x ⬛ 3x ⬛ 3x ⬛ 3x ⬛

Green apple

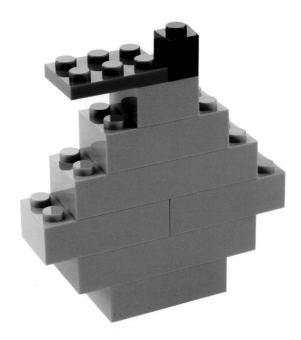

1x  1x

1x 4x 2x

Ghost

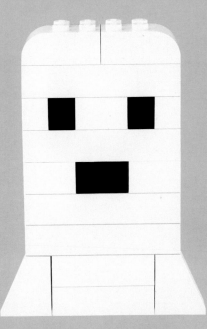

4 x   2 x   2 x   2 x

2 x   1 x   2 x   3 x

Pencil

1x 1x 1x

1x 1x 9x

Candy corn

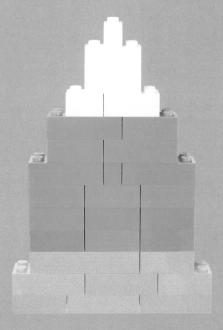

3 x 4 x 1 x 1 x 1 x

3 x 4 x 11 x 1 x

Winter

Snowflake

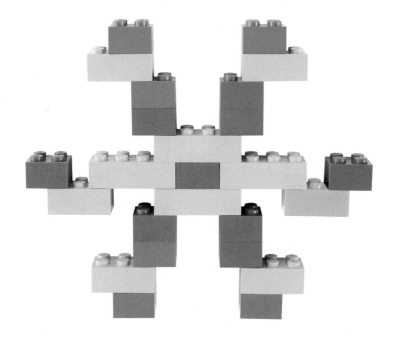

15 x 6 x 4 x

Snowing cloud

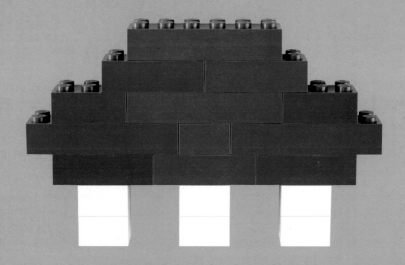

6 x 1 x

2 x 5 x 4 x

Ice skate

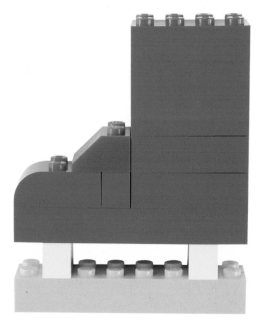

1x 🔵 1x 🔵 1x ⬜

5x 🔵 1x 🔵 2x ⬜ 1x 🔵

Snowy tree

9 x 🟦 4 x 🟦 5 x ⬜

Hot chocolate

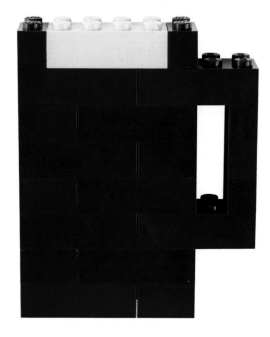

5 x 🧱 5 x 🧱 9 x 🧱 1 x ⬜

Snowman

3 x 🧱 3 x 🧱 1 x 🧱

6 x 🧱 1 x 🧱 6 x 🧱 2 x 🧱

2 x 🧱 3 x 🧱 1 x 🧱

Evergreen tree

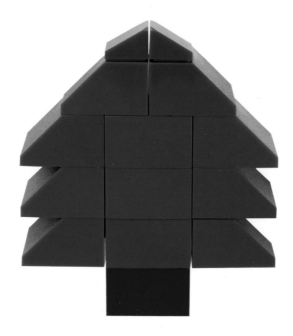

1 x 🧱 3 x 🧱

2 x ◣ 8 x ◥

Candy cane

6 x 🟥 6 x ⬜ 1 x ⬜ 2 x 🟥

Teapot

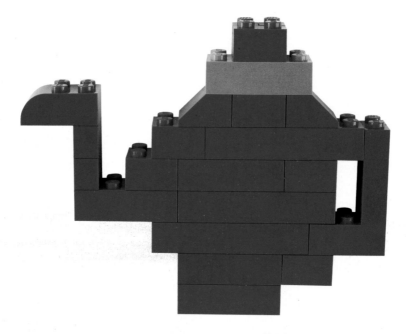

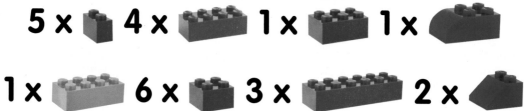

5 x 4 x 1 x 1 x

1 x 6 x 3 x 2 x

Fireplace

9 x   1 x   7 x

1 x   1 x   1 x

Sled

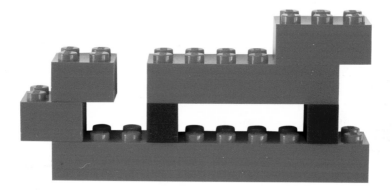

1x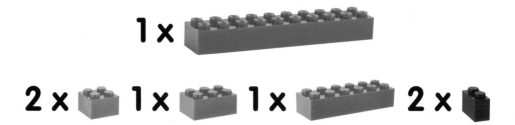

2x 1x 1x 2x

Polar bear

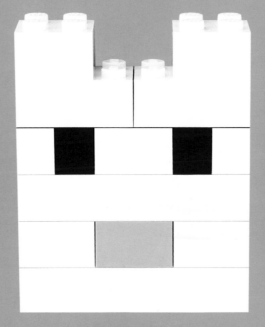

5 x 2 x 2 x

2 x 2 x 1 x

An Imprint of Sterling Publishing Co., Inc.
1166 Avenue of the Americas
New York, NY 10036

ISBN 978-1-4351-6410-9

Manufactured in Guangdong, China.
Lot#:
2 4 6 8 10 9 7 5 3 1
08/16

www.sterlingpublishing.com